Tik-Tik
the Ringtailed Lemur

Authors Alison Jolly and
Hantanirina Rasamimanana
Illustrated by Deborah Ross
Designed by Melanie McElduff

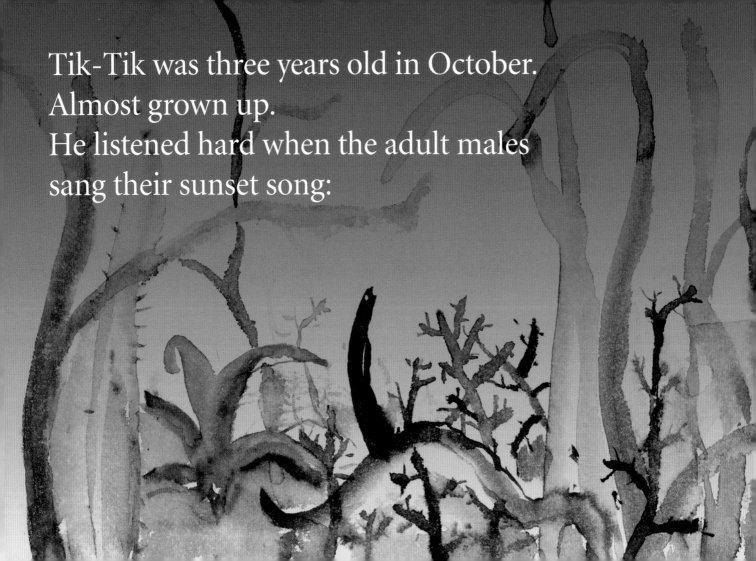

Tik-Tik was three years old in October.
Almost grown up.
He listened hard when the adult males
sang their sunset song:

"Hear me! Hear me!
HEAR ME TOO-OO-OO-OO!

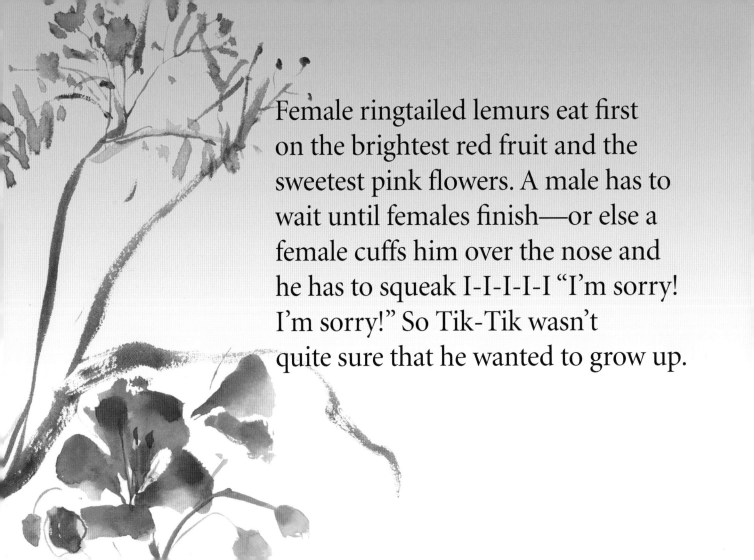

Female ringtailed lemurs eat first on the brightest red fruit and the sweetest pink flowers. A male has to wait until females finish—or else a female cuffs him over the nose and he has to squeak I-I-I-I-I "I'm sorry! I'm sorry!" So Tik-Tik wasn't quite sure that he wanted to grow up.

Instead he play-wrestled with his sister
Maky Mazana. MEW! MEW! called their mother.
"Ready to go?" She was lead female
of the whole troop.

TIK TIK TIK TIK TIK!
"OK! Let's go!" answered all the lemurs.
They set off in a parade.

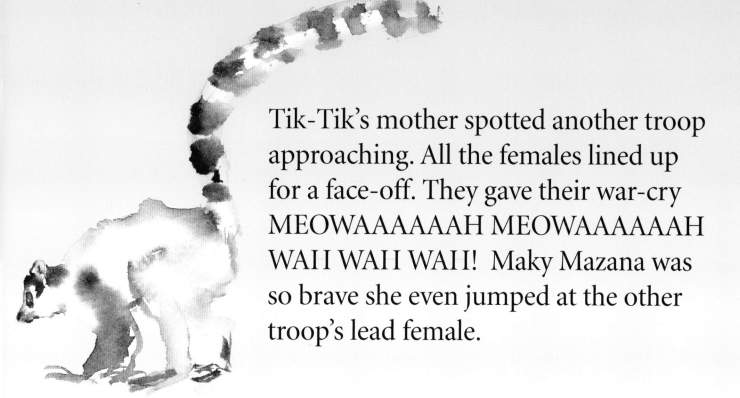

Tik-Tik's mother spotted another troop approaching. All the females lined up for a face-off. They gave their war-cry MEOWAAAAAAH MEOWAAAAAAH WAII WAII WAII! Maky Mazana was so brave she even jumped at the other troop's lead female.

Tik-Tik tried to cross the line. A great big male from the other troop called Longtooth rubbed his tail between his wrist spurs. Then he shook it above his back to send his scent forward: stink-fighting.

Tik-Tik was so frightened that he ran back behind his mother.

But Tik-Tik had picked up the smell of a beautiful female—in the other troop. Her coat was so soft and her tail so full and elegant that her name was Feather-Fur.

Next day Tik-Tik started on a big adventure.

He went out into the spiny forest toward Feather-Fur's troop all on his own. For the first time in his life there was nobody to warn him of danger, going...

WAK WAK WAK at dogs

or SCREEEEAM at hawks.

or TCHK TCHK
TCHK at snakes

A footstep rustled in the leaf litter.
Tik-Tik shot up a spiky octopus tree.

But it was only a radiated tortoise.

A bird flew straight at him.
He was afraid it was a hawk.
He dove head-first into
a needle-needle bush.

No, it was only a hook-billed
vanga defending its nest.

Purple-black clouds grew as tall as mountains
in a greenish sky: the first storm of October.
Lightning bolts crashed all through the forest,
followed by hard, hard hailstones.

Tik-Tik MEOWED and MEOWED and MEOWED
that he was lost. Someone answered MEOW!
He ran back join his troop.

Still, he couldn't get the smell of Feather-Fur out of his head. Next day he set off again, alone.

Maky Mazana wouldn't come with him. They had a new baby sister. Maky Mazana said PURRRRRRR to the baby. Baby sister went PURRRRR right back. Maky Mazana wanted to stay home and become troop leader like their mother.

So Tik-Tik began the loneliest time of his life.
Day after day he sought out Feather-Fur's troop.
Day after day Longtooth and the other males
chased him away.

Finally the troop let him stay,
but he had to walk last in the troop parade
and eat tough old leaves and sour green fruit.
Worst of all, he had to sleep on a tree-branch
all by himself.

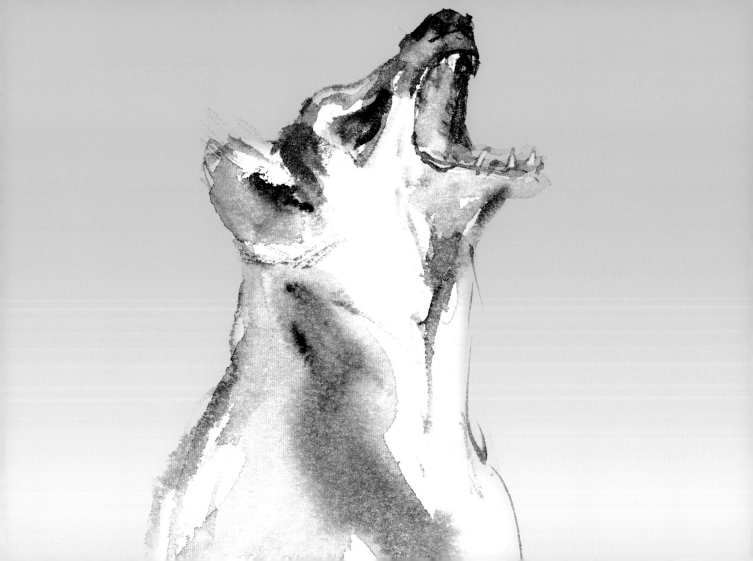

One day in April Feather-Fur began to smell even more beautiful—but all the troop males noticed too. Longtooth rushed at the males and slashed with his sharp canines. One male screamed

EEEEEEEEEEEEEE

and ran away with a big gash in his side. Tik-Tik knew he had to challenge Longtooth.

Tik-tik leaped upward. Longtooth leaped too. Tik-Tik felt a pain in his left ear as Longtooth's canine went through it, but he did not cry out. The males made no noise, just their feet scrabbling in the dust. Tik-tik jumped and dodged and jumped again until the older male was too tired to stop him. He circled round Longtooth to join beautiful Feather-Fur.

Tik-Tik had grown up. And Feather-Fur thought so, too.

And now if you walk in the spiny forest of an evening at sunset, you may hear Tik-Tik singing:

"Hear me too-OO-Oo-oo-oo-oo!"
Oo-OO-Oo-oo-oo-oo!

Ringtailed lemurs can be found within the orange area

ANDRINGITRA

ISALO

BEZA MAHAFALY

ANDOHAHELA

TSIMANAMPETSOTSA

BERENTY